SHADOW PEOPLE

Molly Lynn Watt

Book Design by Steve Glines
Cover Photograph of Aurora Borealis by Molly Lynn Watt
The font used in this text is Garamond.

ISBN: **978-1-4303-0595-8**

Published and Distributed by

Ibbetson Street Press
25 School Street
Somerville, MA 02143
617-628-2313
www.ibbetsonpress.com

LuLu.com

For Danny
and our five grandchildren
Moira, Brian, Lydia, Keely and Alice

Contents

Acknowledgements

Grateful acknowledgment to the following publications where earlier versions of these poems appeared: *Wilderness House Literary Review, HILR Review, Friends Journal, Types and Shadows, Bagels with the Bards, Kent Street Writers Chapbook, Country Dance and Song Society News, Somerville News, Spare Change.*

Special gratitude to Fred Marchant, Eva Bourke, Fran Vaughan, Macdara Woods, Jane Eklund, Jane Katims and H. Susan Freireich for generosity, leading me out of bewilderment into experimentation, encouraging new growth and reading early drafts.

Total Gratitude to my lifeline of poet colleagues and supporters at the Bagel Bard's breakfast conversations on Saturday mornings, the William Joiner Center for the Study of War and Social Consequences at University of Massachusetts Boston, Fireside Readings at Cambridge Cohousing, HILR study groups, Poets of the Roundtable at Harvard, the Writers and Artists Group at Cambridge Friends Meeting, Every Other Friday Group, Thursday Morning Group, Divers and Kent Street Writers.

Thanks to Doug Holder and Dianne Robitaille of Ibbetson Street Press and to Steve Glines of Industrial Myth & Magic for supporting me and the production of this book and for all they do every day for poets throughout the Greater Boston area and beyond the beyond.

Deepest love and thanks to Dan Lynn Watt for supporting me and the process from start to finish with intelligent insight, good humor, good food, editorial and technical assistance.

Introduction

Molly Lynn Watt is not only the gregarious host of the popular "Fireside Reading Series," in Cambridge, Massachusetts but an accomplished poet in her own right. Watt is all about striking imagery; whether describing the Aurora Borealis as a seductive, flashy lady of the night, or the emergence of a sultry Billy Holiday from a cloud of enigmatic cigarette smoke; we are hooked, and like any self-respecting addict, we are looking to score our next fix of her beguiling work.

Doug Holder/ Ibbetson Street Press

Aurora Borealis

We've become night travelers
creeping along Alaskan highways
for one more chance encounter.
She—beguiling hooker
draped in ruby satins—
flashes along Earth's silhouette
doing hijinks across the skies
dazzling frost crystals in riverbeds
whispering to crackling ground
to join her juicy dance—
then ripples on.

We are shadow people
stalking her by moonlight
desirous of another glimpse
as she rides the mountain ridges.
We'll wait all night for one caress
from her expanding waves of sheen.
But she's a neon flirt
who swirls and flares
cavorting through celestial skies—
a good-time girl—
she soars alone.

Tumartat Pieces

Tumartat is the gathering of pieces of anything and putting them together to make a whole. Walkie Charles, Emmonak, Alaska

The elders sit on the floor folding and refolding
They use no measuring tools, eyeballing until satisfied
folding once lengthwise, once across the width.
One hand holds the corner of double folds
the other makes a single scissor cut.
If done precisely—
the way their wrinkled fingers know—
a perfect rhombus and four triangles
slide to the floor.

Lilly Afcan lays down otter, wolf and calf skins
for teachers-in-training to cover edge to edge
with paper shapes, cut, trace
sew with dental floss sinew
into headdresses for dancing
to Elias Polty's drumbeats
and Theresa Mike's throaty song
retelling Annie Blue's Yup'ik tale:

Molly Lynn Watt

A long time ago
grandmother sees village children
ridicule her granddaughter.
She makes a doll, gifts it on the girl's palm
sings in her ear yug-aa-aa-naq-aa-aa.
The girl and doll rise to the heavens
 becoming ageskurpak—the brightest morning star
everyone will look up to and admire.

The elders and teachers are braiding tumartat pieces
a present for their children to become ageskupaks, bright stars.
They sing them on their way, *yug-aa-aa-naq-aa-aa.*

Note: *Tumartat* is pronounced in the Yup'ik language *too-mucch-tut* and
Ageskurpak is pronounced as *ah-gis-ucch-buk.*

3

Mendenhall Glacier

A misting May morn bald eagle circle
skunk cabbage unfurl blue lupine glow
magpie flit among the spruce
tourists scuttle to book tours   see it all
we lace on hiking boots   pack knapsacks
take Juneau public transit number four.

The glacier's been advancing and retreating
three thousand years or more
we wait forty-five minutes for a bus
ride an hour with folks bandying news
hopping off to grocery shop   totem carve
fish   drop the kids at school.

We trek two-miles through rain forest
wind song and mosquitoes
round the bend to snow-topped mountains
engorged valleys   blue-iced melt-water
flares down Nugget Falls to meet
its mirror-image in the lake below.

Where icebergs float   loons swim
artic terns and brown bears feed
we scan for salmon spawning
examine wet bear tracks   follow a porcupine
into the shadow of the glacier   first named Auke
in honor of the Tlinqit People.

We hike to places woolly mammoths roamed
before the Ice Age shrouded earth in miles of floe
still melting groaning to our feet.
The glacier is unstable without warning
it may crack up calve chunks the size of buildings
generate wave surges cold enough to kill.

Despite everything Mendenhall Glacier
and the Tlinqit First People are still here.
We stand beside what nature's giant plow
ground to dust emulsified in glacial water
cascading hundreds of miles thousands of years
to lap our boots and rush away.

We hear the raven kaa.

February 2005

Encrusted snow banks
   frost heaves blighted melt
we ache for hyacinth forsythia
   for spring

At first light we drive 200 miles
   to leafless Central Park
      acres of orange curtains hang from Gates
   billow above snow

Backlit by sun
   people stroll in saffron fashions
      boots wool coats dyed hair
   dogs in yellow jackets strain at leashes
children hide and shriek
   youth on rocks smoke dope
      a saxophone player beneath a footbridge
      blows tunes
        strangers dance
          painters paint
        venders pitch their wares
     tee shirts bill caps hotdogs balloons

Beside the duck pond
   people hear the story of the red tailed hawk's eviction
     from his nest on stone cherubim
      a public outcry a cause célèbre

Molly Lynn Watt

Pale wings soar translucent against the burnt orange sky
    people point and cheer
        towers forever falling in my mind
            reframe as veils of marigold embraces
                for people on a February walk
            rooting for one lone hawk's return to nest

Note: Christo and Jeanne-Claude's installation, *Gates*, Central Park, New York City, February 12-27, 2005.

Lord God Bird

We live between two worlds
hunting grubs and seeking sky
wanting proof we did no harm
we quest the holy grail of birds
presumed extinct for 60 years
we leap at news
from a bayou deep in Arkansas
impenetrable by light
Scientists sitting in canoes
glimpsed   or may have glimpsed
the ivory-billed woodpecker
flying to a nest in silver limbs
heard it hammering out
a rap of solitary freedom
before Lord God Bird
spreads giant wings
for eternal fields of light

Pub Dance

Dancing with you
is not hip-wrenching twists
as we gyrate to a flashing strobe
under a moon of mirrors.
Nor do we slow-grope to heaven
under crepe-paper streamers
in a chaperoned gym.
It's to the UM-pa-pa of the polka
played on the jukebox for a quarter
your hands brace my hips
my arms encircle your neck
we—the only dancers—grind
sawdust up at the Golden Eagle Pub.

Partner Swing

You in a tee-shirt—me in a flare skirt—
tap our toes to the beat of the bass
the prompter calls *honor your partner*
we're off in a fervor of pulse and whirl
join hands four to form a star
promenade down and come back home—
we *pass over—* they *pass under—*
clasp hands across for lady's chain
the flute notes fly—we *weave a basket*
the birdie hops in—the crow hops after
the piano keeps a steady beat
everyone dips—everyone dives
partners *gypsy along the line—*
a hint of jitterbug—a smatter of swing
a tat-tat-tat—a fling-fling-fling
we glisten and grin as the dance ends
with a *partner swing.*

1938

That bloody year of 1938 when I was born
A rainbow bridge fell like a wounded serpent to the snow
I witnessed the hurricane without a name from mother's arms

Paul Robeson roused anti-fascist Spain with song
Laura Ingalls Wilder wrote of home by Plum Creek's flow
That bloody year of 1938 when I was born

Broadway raved of Thornton Wilder's play *Our Town*
Errol Flynn played Robin Hood and redistributed dough
I witnessed the hurricane without a name from mother's arms

Judy Garland's debut brought her fans, much later they would mourn
Pearl Buck won the Nobel Prize for *The Good Earth*'s sorrow
That bloody year of 1938 when I was born

Nazis carried out pogroms against the Jewish born
Ferdinand Porsche built the people's car for masses on the go
I witnessed the hurricane without a name from mother's arms

Storm troopers smashed synagogues and shops and homes
Time named Hitler man of the year, not freedom's foe
That bloody year of 1938 when I was born
I witnessed the hurricane without a name from mother's arms

Dead

1

Tony, sandy-haired cocker
warmer than Grandma's rag quilt
let out in a blizzard, found cold in a pit
icicles gripped his fur
I shouted his name
he didn't budge
I poked at his side
it was hard as a board
Dead
The first time I saw dead
touched dead, wept after dead
Night after night I wailed
loss into my pillow
My father said, let her be
she's a little widow
tossing in a hollow bed.

2

Verna Jean's baby brother
born a funny shape
We were too young
and never saw him in his hospital crib
Verna Jean told me, they feed him
through a tube cut into his gut
Her mother said, all that boy does is cry
She cried when she said it
One day that baby brother turned blue
then dead
Grown-ups carried flowers to church
Me and Verna Jean hid under the porch
listening to the organ music
playing with the jar of honey
my mother sent to sweeten death

All afternoon we turned the jar over and over
watching the bubble rise up to Jesus.

3
One day the postman brought a package
wrapped in brown paper, tied up with string
I opened to find a Japanese doll
dressed in the first kimono I'd seen
cradled in a silk-lined lacquered box
Before I wrote to thank him
Hubert came home from Korea
in a box draped with a flag—dead.
Once I'd met him at a band concert
but refused to kiss him
saying, when I'm older.

4
The first day on my first job as a nurse's aide
I answered the call bell of the jaundiced woman
propped her onto the cold metal bedpan
listened for the sound that did not come
not even a hum of breath
I felt for pulse—just like that she was dead.
I vomited all afternoon thinking I'd killed her—
not remembering her chart said terminal.

5
My father and I set tea for the few Presbyterians
still worshipping in Newark
placed lilacs in the chancel
How tiny my 92-year-old grandma looked
lying dead in the satin-lined coffin
dressed in her gray Sunday best
pearl earrings, silver brooch

thin white braids crowned her head
How pink her cheeks as if rouged by the wind
My father held her wrinkled hands in his
slipped her wedding band from her finger
passing it along to me
She'd raised five children alone
selling the mahogany dining table
the upright piano, the family homestead
I turned grandma's ring round and round—
not the thin heft of gold
she'd entertained me with long ago—
this was a brass fake thing.

Molly Lynn Watt

Song of Laundry

Rain taps the windowpane
time wilts back as I fold laundry still dryer warm
smoothing tee shirts   pairing socks   stacking linens
across our king-sized bed covered in hues of blue
a log cabin quilt pattern cut from clothing
once dancing down creek beds on backs of children
clothes washed and dried in Appalachian breezes

Time wilts back to summers spent
along the Na-ro-me-ok-na-hoo-sank-a-tank-shunk Brook
pounding stains with rocks in clear spring water
stringing the family washing out to dry on trees
as Wampanoag women did before us in this place

Time wilts back to Granny in a straw hat
wringing out the family wash   pinning each garment
on lines strung between the maples   pairs of socks hung by toes
brassieres and rayon panties hiding under diapers
bed-sheet ghosts gathering up the scent of clover
Papa's Sunday shirt bobs like a Morris Dancer's capers

Time wilts back to Mondays   the universal washday
riding in the backseat of my parents' Chevrolet
past the farms of neighbors
Father reading out the laundry news
Diapers, that baby's finally come
Too much bedding   they've got the grippe
Lace tablecloth   no overalls   Death or relatives came calling

Artists of the wash loads displayed on lines have faded out
we do the laundry inside not caring if it rains or snows
no easy way of knowing what goes on behind drawn shades
when a visit over tea or a pot of chicken soup is needed
You can't find this kind of news in the *Sunday Times*

15

Eyes

He leans on the handle of his hoe, between the bean hills.
He's chopped back the weeds, spread manure over the roots.
He lifts his eyes to the apple trees planted a dozen years before.
His eyes are a dance of blue.

                                    I want to write about those eyes—
eyes that say with one gaze *I like you.*
Those eyes talk to everyone he meets.
The eyes say *I respect your work* to the man replacing a fan belt.
The eyes say *I care* to the parishioner weeping after death's visit.
The eyes say *I love you* to his wife lighting candles at the supper table.
The eyes say *I'm proud* to his son freshening the heifer's hay.
When his daughter jumps from the school bus her pigtails flying
the eyes become a liquid steel pausing
            where her sweater pulls tight across her chest
            running down her bare legs.

She feels shame tap her shoulder, *hasn't he seen legs before?*
She feels funny, tugs her skirt to cover up her knees
            runs to the kitchen lit by firelight
            drops her sweater to the floor
            slumps in a chair
            hardly breathing at her mother's table.

                                    But her mother isn't there.
She watches his freckled hands opening the icebox
setting out a glass of milk, a dish of applesauce he's made.
The eyes meet hers, but now, in that dim room
they're like a sunset in July.
He says *missed you, glad you're home.*

16

She lets out the breath she's been holding
grabs the glass of milk, the dish of applesauce
rushes out, slams the door behind—
anything to stop his eyes from stalking her with love
      leaving her to dread the night ahead
      when she will kneel to say her prayers, as she always has
      he will wait to tuck her in, the way he always does
      smooth the covers shaping them around her body
      lay his head upon her breast
      linger too long to cuddle and to kiss.
She will not shut her eyes all night
her eyes stand sentry to her fears.

Stone 1948

Smooth, round and mottled—
this stone from the beach we ran to each day
far from fights between parents
and worries of bombings and war

We carved caves from sand dunes
dined on beach peas and plums
lay under the sky on beds molded from sand
lulled by a duet of wind across waves

Each day we returned with shovels and pails
to that pebble-streaked place on the shore
bent to the task of rebuilding escape
until cowbells jangled and summoned us home

The stone and I — both smooth, round and mottled
were tumbled by wind   polished by sand
the stone on my sill looks just as it did
but silently signals how far I ran

Survival Practice 1945

We called it Contest Time
in the oak and maple woods
where we gathered up dead branches
built up forts   shared scraps of food
stolen from our parents rationed tables

This was where we really lived
eating mishmash from chipped china
taking naps on planks turned silver
mastering matches   torching brush
worshiping fire turn wood to embers

We knew enough to turn our buttocks
unzip dungarees   I   the only girl
grabbed up my tummy   on the cry of three
we spun about letting loose a giant stream
slipped home in time for supper

Lady Day 1958

Waitstaff
moving through eddies of smoke
extinguish all cigarettes
A hush moves through the crowd
as a woman enters
a gardenia behind her ear
a white satin gown
too loose for her frame
She leans on the arm of an escort
making her way to the stage
A bit unsteady, she turns
her ringed hands limp at her waist
(no hint of finger-snapping tonight)
she stares over the crowd
dignified and expressionless
as houselights dim
to a single stream on her haggard face
She opens her ruby mouth
a low dry hoarse voice drips out
word after word
until the room is flooded
Southern trees bear a strange fruit
Blood on the leaves and blood at the root

Billie Holliday, head high, eyes closed
puts Jim Crow on stage
I am a witness beside her
standing under the poplar trees
I am the lynching party
I am the body swinging in the breeze
I am not breathing and my heart is breaking
as Lady Day burns out word after word
scorching the souls gathered in the darkness
Here is a strange and bitter crop

and Lady stops
the song is done
the entertainment over
the houselights blare up
I see Lady sway a little
All patrons remain frozen in place
Lady's escort takes her arm
helps her from the stage
someone starts to clap
another joins in
and another
until the whole room is applauding
as Lady Day walks away

Note: Billie Holiday, nicknamed Lady Day, was born April 7, 1915 named
Eleanora Fagan, died at age 44 on July 17, 1959, nine months after the
concert. The song *Strange Fruit*, written by Abel Meeropol, became her
signature song.

Enumerating

I plug a quarter in the meter
to give me half an hour
there still are twenty minutes
before the post office will close
I am carrying a package
a present for my sister
who will celebrate her birthday
across the Atlantic Ocean
I'm the last to join the line
to wait a turn at the counter
to account for the contents
of the parcel I will send
I fill out a Customs Declaration
on the old Form C
the postal clerk instructs me
to redo it on the new one 2-9-3
I must list the weights and values
give a clear directive
in the case of unanticipated non-delivery
Should it be abandoned, redirected
or should they simply send it back to me
I have wrapped three books
for my one and only sister
each one has a twin that lives with me
I decide they total up at three pounds
I refuse to deal in ounces
and estimate their value
at twenty dollars each   times three
The clerk scans in the bar code
figures up the tally owed
I plunk down loose coins
adding up to sixteen bucks
I fill out the forms in triplicate
to reveal where I live

usually identified by its yellow door
but in the allotted boxes all that fits
is the numeral 3-1-5
street and number
plus the nine digit zip
I'm getting pretty frantic
I've used up 18 minutes
I glance outside and spy
a meter maid passing by
The postal clerk turns off the lights
puts the keys in the locks
zips his leather jacket up
to leave for the night
I've just written out
the *from* parts and
haven't started writing
my gift is *to* dear Annie
who is living on an island
which is part of County Cork
and is off the coast of Ireland.
To go there   take a ferry
then head straightway up the hill
to Bridgie's House
There'll be no trouble finding it
they all know where Annie lives
To send my little package
on its three thousand mile trip
to a sheep path on this Irish-speaking isle
I don't need to write more numbers
I can almost taste the salt air
feel the ferry rock beneath me
hear the shrieking of the gulls
the clanging of the buoys

Shadow People

I wish I'd mailed myself
to sit near Annie in the sky
taking birthday tea
where the fairies still reside
looking down the rock-strewn bullig
to where the whales and dolphins frolic

The clerk jerks me from my reverie
by passing a receipt to me
stating the date and fees I've paid
I head back to my car
find a ticket on the windshield
indicating a fifteen dollar fine
for five minutes parking overtime

Margie (1916-1999)

It is always spring where she sits in her chair
under Monet's blue sky and fields of tulips
Her fragile body bends over the nail clippers
moving them toward her empty hand   shaking
both hands shaking   she misses and starts over
intent on making her right hand meet her left
Again she misses   looks up at the still windmill in oil
her face relaxing into a faraway smile
I went to see the tulips   she says to no one in particular
Every day I cut a dozen for the table

She remembers me
sitting with her for another afternoon
the dream fades from her face
she stands and leaves without comment
Long ago she trimmed my husband's fingernails
when he was too young to work the clippers
burying the parings among her tulip bulbs
I want to gather her hands in mine
clip her yellowed finger nails grown hard
fly her to Holland   lay her in a petal bed

Nothing Of Value

There's nothing of value here
we can leave, my mother said
at the door of his hospital room
The dishes stacked high, the coffee long cold
bed linens rumpled, drawn all the way back
air smelled of urine and pine scented soap
the IV dangled in a tangled loop

There's nothing of value here, she said
tucking hair to her bun   her purse to her bosom
she thanked the nurses for all they had done
We talked a bit as I drove her home
about their last days spent reminiscing
driving back roads filled with ghost traces
of raising four kids in their chosen town

We've left nothing of value, she said again
Your father is gone, and now I'm alone
Then she got on the phone to share the news
arrange the funeral, and do all the business
that keeps one so busy when a loved one dies
It takes all your courage, it takes all your focus
to just follow through on the things you must do

And when she was finished, she went up to rest
on the double bed she'd shared with him
for fifty years of loving and fighting
for fifty years she'd heard him breathing
while she read detectives long into the night
worried with children awakened in fright
He served her coffee each morning in bed

Molly Lynn Watt

With her Lover's Knot coverlet over her shoulders
The scent of him lingering all around
his King James Bible in place at the bedside
the gallery of grandchildren smiling at her
It was here her tears began to flow
she cursed at God for stealing him home
and leaving her here to live on alone

Into The Crack Of Dawn

No one placed a gardenia
on her bedside table

No one set a pillow just so
beneath her head

No one sat beside her
to lull her with a ballad or read

Corinthians from the King James Bible.
She lay alone in bed

Alone—unless you count
the French clock chiming out the hours

or snow whipping at the window panes
or Blacky barking by the door

or father's ghost come to serve
her coffee in a red ware mug

She said, *I'll only be a second*
rose and brushed her hair

dabbed lipstick on her mouth
Chanel behind her ears

and father took her in his arms
and said, *they're on their own*

He waltzed her like a bride
into the crack of dawn

Molly Lynn Watt

Spring Egg Hunt

My granddaughter Lydia
wears cherry blush and lip-gloss
and stands three inches taller than I
She tosses back her raven hair
doubtful she'll participate

The weather-report says rain
but my neighbor Julie and I
hide three hundred plastic eggs
in the shade garden   among the stand
of birch saplings in the glade
along the commuter tracks

The rain holds off

Lydia on platform shoes
whirls across the grass
trailed by two-dozen neighbor children
scooping plastic eggs from hiding places
into gaudy basket imports from China

> *A decade earlier*
> *under gnarled apple boughs*
> *coming into blossom*
> *Lydia carried an Appalachian basket*
> *running after older cousins*
> *gathering hard-boiled eggs*
> *dyed mustard yellow with onion skins*
> *robin's egg blue with cabbage leaves*
> *eggs laid by my mother's hens*
> *It snowed that Easter at my mother's*
> *the last day my mother lived*
> *the first death Lydia remembers*
> *Three days later*

Shadow People

in the shadow of the Celtic Cross
Lydia threw rose petals over
her great-grandmother's red ware urn
handmade by my brother

Today Lydia straddles the garden wall
empties jelly beans and candy kisses
from her basket filled with neon eggs
gifting them to the youngest
glances up and says *Grams,*
next year I'll hide the eggs

Molly Lynn Watt

Walking With Alice

Alice wants to walk the dirt road
officially it's spring
We watch snowflakes floating past the windowpanes
listen to the water drip dripping from the gutter
We pull on fleeces
but won't make more concessions to chilly air
wanting the sun to whisper in our ears spring's come

Alice dances up the ridges
prances through the puddles
stomps poems with her sneakers
tosses pebbles into songs

I plod along behind her
searching budded twigs
I need proof spring's come

Alice scoops up fallen oak leaves
the snow melted and they've come back to me

I'm too busy seeking signs of new life
and don't care about her dead leaves

She's gathered up a bouquet
waves it for the sun to see
the snow melted and they've come back to me
She throws the leaves up high
fluttering with them to the ground

I ignore her miracle looking for a robin
. or a flying insect or a pollywog in water

Let's find frogs, Grandma
How can they breathe underneath the ground?

31

Shadow People

When will they come alive again?

Alice takes a stick and pokes it in the dirt
She forms the letters of her name
A – L – I – C – E
proclaiming for the world to see
she learned to write her name this winter
Now you write yours, Grandma

I do   it feels like the most important writing anyone can do

I cut budded twigs
Alice calls them *fat*
they must be pregnant like the cat

She can't imagine they will bloom
but is patient while I keep collecting
then flies like a siren in the wind
back to the door where
Gus   her yellow lab   is waiting
Do you have a dog, Grandma?

I tell her Tony, my cocker spaniel
and his successor, Suzy, are both long dead

*Will they come back
like the brown leaves and flowers?*

I shake my head

Alice, quiet for a moment, perks up
*Gus is leaning on your lap because
his grandma's dead
So you can be his grandma
and he can be your dog*
she pats him on the head

I place the budded twigs in water
stand the vase beside her bed
She arranges brittle oak leaves
in a glass placed by the vase and says
the buds are getting live again
and the leaves are getting deader

More Questions

The angel of death stalks night
three thousand years later
as family and friends reunite
at the Passover Seder
blessing wine—the force of life
dipping karpas in salty tears
retelling of plagues and strife
hopes for freedom over the years

Youngsters ask four questions—plus more
Why are folks poor? Why are folks dying?
Why is there war? Why is government lying?
Will bombings ever cease?
Will Elijah bring promised peace?
Every head turns to the open door

Molly Lynn Watt

Aspiration

Confetti snow
danced into collapsing black holes
debris filled syringe after syringe
until the shadows
on the doctor's face fell away
and the lab technician said
releasing my breast
from the plexiglass vise
for the fifth time that month
You're ok again—
don't slip on black ice
I tossed the johnny into the bin of ghosts
stepped into pelting sleet—
exhaling

Elegy to a Failed Marriage

A firecracker ignited by your spark
Last summer's log fed to your flames
The crystal glass stomped by your boot

Your heart's desire
petrified in blame
reduced to ash and soot

Ever After

What can I say to my friend when he phones to say
he is filing for divorce from his second wife?

I will listen as he speaks in even tones
as if this is a rational decision
made by adding up the debits and deposits
at each month's end and concluding
after years in the red
to stem his losses
close down the account

He will not recall his aching groin
yearning for a lover
how he found her shining in the sky
flew her to his meadow
built a palace out of logs
to breathe the nights away together

He will remember only
how he tried to banish father's angry ghost
call forth warmth from his withholding mother
How he stretched to wrap his bride in love
but parental ghosts kept stalking
he couldn't stop their voices
from inhabiting his head

He tried to stuff them in the closet
drown them in the well
burn them in the wood stove
The ghosts were undeterred
and simply stayed and raged
at all his hopes and imperfections
until his palace transformed to a cage
and his wife became his father
and he became his mother

Shadow People

My friend will not howl
his sorrows to the skies
He will not shave his head
nor rend his garments into rags
Instead he'll flee his lover
and that dark fortress in the meadow
while his mother ghost and father ghost
ride forever ever after
tethered to his side

Molly Lynn Watt

On Cambridge Common

Students hustle by but do not see him
alone on the park bench taking a smoke
Years ago he was a student on his way to somewhere
Now he spends his days on the Common
his silver hair pulled out of the way in a pony-tail
always the same frayed jeans and shirt
gray sneakers tied with string
A canvas case patched with duct tape sits beside him
he lifts out a battered 12-string guitar
its bridge stressed out from years of percussive picking—
glances at the faint autographs on its leather back strap
Josh White, Guy Carawan, Pete Seeger, Tony Saletan—
places his still-burning cigarette between two strings
adjusts the tuning pegs, strums to find a key
hums as his feet tap out the beat and sings
This world is not my home, I'm just a-passing through…

His lips curl into a smile around the sounds
as he sings to a galaxy of ghosts
He is not worrying about sifting through trash cans
for discarded chips, half-eaten sandwiches
nor finding a place to sleep on a bench, behind a bush
or with some young woman happening his way
willing to share her dorm bed for a night of song
Tomorrow he will drift off to another bench
shrouded in the proud tradition of protest
to rage against hard times, lost causes, corrupt bosses
mine disasters, union strikes, unjust wars, parted lovers
not thinking of the wife and babies he left behind
He pauses for a nip from his monogrammed flask
The angels beckon me from Heaven's open door
And I can't feel at home in this world anymore…

Song of Consuming
After Walt Whitman's *Song of Myself*

I celebrate consuming
and what I consume you may consume, too
for every item belonging to me can as well belong to you.

I ordered the sand washed shirts and cargo pants
in tarragon and vintage rose that machine wash and dry
to wear while walking the gentle slopes of Danehy Park.

I charged the durable lagoon blue sandals
with nubuck straps and rubber outsoles for traction
to journey along the gray cement and redbrick sidewalks to Harvard Square.

I craved the shape solver bathing suit
with three times the stretch and slimming in periwinkle and eggplant
to swim laps at Cambridge Rindge and Latin High School pool.

I bought the tankini
with supportive softcups and conservative leg openings in plum and cherry
to sit and sun on my four-foot deck overlooking the commuter rail.

I wear the summer breeze tees and adventure pants
with zip vents and invisible pockets in skylight and ink blue
to ride the escalator down two building tiers to board the Redline T.

After I lose ten pounds I will squeeze into a pair of pencil-cut faded jeans
with angled pockets and spandex for a forgiving fit
to circle Fresh Pond counting mallards.

Failing to receive a mail order catalog
be encouraged to access one by internet
and you can consume, too.

Riversing 2004

On the red-rimmed eve of equinox
rowers bend silver oars
embroidering the river surface
measuring off the days
before brisker air will come
Cyclists weave through
students reclining on the grass
children laugh as
quailing geese take off
flying through the footbridge
a mirror-image to the river flow

No more harvest hoe-downs on the Charles
or barn-raisings before snows appear
we gather at river goddess Oshun's bidding
to sing as she extends giant puppet arms
conducting a thousand singers
lined along the river banks
in volleys of quadraphonic harmonies
uniting two cities with a bridge of song

Redline

1
leaving
drips of spilled milk on the table
grains of muesli on the floor
half a cup of coffee in the mug
obituaries open on the chair

2
hurry hurry hurry down 3 flights of stairs
along the street
two stories down the escalator
to wait wait wait
the old man calls
Spare Change, get your Spare Change

3
the outbound is running 1-2-3 in a row
I check my watch, I'm inbound
at least   I mean to be

4
the banjo lets fly a Celtic jig
I throw a quarter in the case
stare down the track
check my watch
and wait

5
eeeeeerrrrrrrrkkkkkk crick
the doors spring back
one seat
I press past others to snag it
stopping at a pool of yellow

Molly Lynn Watt

6
I stand

7
a woman holds an apple core
a man replacing double-A batteries
drops one, says oh shit and leaves
a pregnant woman carries
a baby in a snuggly-bag
no one rises to offer her a seat

8
everyone has somewhere to go
everyone has something to do
the T emerges from underground
but no one looks to see
a rainbow arching over
rowers on the Charles
or the community sailing fleet

9
I could get my G.E.D.
have a three-week vacation in a hospital
earn a fifteen hundred dollar stipend
be counseled about my unwanted pregnancy
join Hope Fellowship in worship
be surprised by Michelob light
get tested for HIV
so many ways to mend my life

10
everyone is studying feet
or listening to an ipod
or diddling with a cell phone
or reading
heels click across the floor
a man taps his walking stick

against people's toes
people press each other
against the *Do Not Lean on this Door* sign
ding ding ding
grrrrrrrrrrrrr grrrrrrrrrr grrrrrrrrr

11
seven cups of Dunkin' Donuts
nine cups of Starbucks
eight Evian water bottles
everyone's hydrating
no one's relating

12
Porter
Harvard
Central
Kendall
Charles/MGH
Park
Downtown Crossing
South Station
Broadway
Andrews
JFK/UMASS
my half-hour mantra
to the rhythms of the T
takes me from home
to where I need to be

Molly Lynn Watt

Portraits for Peace 1964

The white haired woman in red
sits beside the children's climbing tree
in the Friends Meeting garden
holding a drawing pad and pencil
A sign says *portraits for peace - $1*

Children play tag through conversations
toss rings to the nose of a clown
blow bubbles from clay pipes
survey dolls and trucks fixed-up to sell
eat rice krispie treats   drink iced lemonade

Someone has an aquarium of hamsters
hold for a penny, take home for a dime
No one pauses for a portrait
I lead my four-year-old by the hand
sit her in front of the woman in red

She folds back her pad and draws
the outline of my daughter's head
a shadowy smudge   webs of lines
fullness   depth   face   hair   gazing eyes
my daughter is reborn through her pencil

I take my two-year-old by the hand
she looks a little proud   sits tall   sits still
mesmerized into an hour of meditation
the woman sketches out her soul
as friends fly by   laughing   teasing

The woman in red seems to
glow quietness to my daughters
from deep within her being
unlike our experience in Quaker Meeting—
the girls fidgeting through the hour of worship

45

Shadow People

Later I learn the woman   as a girl
petted bees that did not try to fly away
as a mother   she enthralled her daughters
with painted Easter eggs   secret lives of flowers
art books at the breakfast table

Not content painting Chinese vases in pretty settings
she traveled into operating rooms
city streets and country landscapes
pulling tensions out   simplifying lines
painting by natural light

For her hundredth birthday
wheeled in to her gallery show
to celebrate with family and fans
her eyesight dimmed   she joked
I've traded sight for in-sight

Today Polly Thayer Starr's art
hangs in the MFA
The Fogg Museum
and   on my bedroom wall
but that day in 1964

she drew peace
peace in the world
peace in art
peace in one's heart
all parts of the same thing

Molly Lynn Watt

Self Portrait Though A Camera Lens

After reading *Self Portrait in a Convex Mirror* by John Ashbery and
viewing *Saga: The Journey of Arno Rafael Minkkinen.*

1

Arno Rafael Minkkinen captured with a camera
one foot and a partial leg   his own
a foot thrust up through crystalline snow
echoing the surround of ice-glazed grasses
back-lit by winter sun and bent by weight and wind.
The viewer comes across this scene decades later
saved in a picture of black and white and silver tones
and feels the cold of winter and its sun-lit heat
and knows she views no disembodied part, no macabre murder scene.
Blood pulses through that foot's flesh-tones.
The perspective on this field is close,
a frozen moment where someone she cannot see
reclines on mother earth, although she does not see the earth
nor question her belief. It's there, but out of sight, a mystery.
Instead she wonders about the photographer,
well, about the man
she has forgotten he's designer and recorder of his fate
the man must be lying beneath a comforter of snow
although she sees not much more than one protruding foot
she knows in certainty, he's there.

2

The viewer scrolls along Arno's Saga of a Journey
shown by one hundred and twenty self-portraits
in 20 by 24-inch frames.
She pauses before two hands
well   really not two hands at all.
Really just the fingers of two hands
emerging from the lake
each bowing toward the other.
Really just the first fingers of the hands are visible

47

and the second fingers only glimpsed
but the viewer knows fingers three, four and five
exist inside the arching digits
juxtaposed against shadows become circles
and suggest childhood play-binoculars to the viewer
used to focus on what is far away.
She looks beyond the hands
that are not hands   but are
to see the fullness of the sun
well, fullness partially obscured by cloud
and feels the blueness of the water shown in grays
rippling outward in concentric circles
and only later realizes she'd looked over, not through the finger lenses
and filled out the circle forms in her imagination
from some segments shaped like furling fingers.
By what mystery she can not say
she felt crisp airy air and flowing watery water
held for years by tones of blacks and whites on photo paper.
She only knew she recognized that place   distorted in perspective
where fingers are larger than the pond and sun
and from one foot's gesture she'd brought forth a naked man.

3
The viewer stops to see a third frame
where two feet touch down on water
a right foot   well, the ball of the right foot only
and a left foot follows   really just the big toe touches down
as the legs   stopped below the knees
stand taller than the spit of land beyond
the pond he's walking on in 1974.
The viewer finds him there, still walking, in 2005.
It's eerie wondering, is he walking on the water
and what that might mean as he treads and clicks
his way around the world in photos he's staged in nature
one man begetting himself in natural places in light and dark on paper.
I no longer think of Arno, the man, naked on a public beach
creating repeated magic tricks of disappearing

from police and upset neighbors
for his instant of time and place selected for one camera's take.
His image stopped   while in full motion   moving over, toward, along.
I think instead of skinny-dipping in the summer
long romps barefoot in the sand, of being nude in nature.
I feel air and sun and rain and rock and grass and space
my unencumbered body connecting with my lover's.
I, too, may well be treading on the water
looking through a lens of air
holding up a foot-flag in winter toward the sun —
I recognize I can't impose permanence on footsteps —
an earlier distortion of perspective —
I am serene, while viewing Arno's Saga
while treading air and wondering
about ripples I write on paper moving on
beyond my sight, beyond my reach, away from knowing.

Weary Peace Warrior

I am sick of pelting snow and sleet
my stuffy nose and freezing feet
I'm tired from marches waging peace
though I'm well practiced
drawing words on signs
and passing leaflets out

I'm a warrior using chants and shouts
for large ideals I care about
like justice and democracy
I'm worn down from life as one long vigil
cracking at hypocrisies
and hoping this will keep us free

I'm ready for a shift of gaze
I'll watch for sunshine through the haze
dappling light across the path
waking lady slippers in the glade
warming turtles laying eggs
illuminating monarchs' flights

I'll listen for the rainstorm and its thunder
laugh out loud   renewed with wonder
then thrust another banner up that wars will cease

Molly Lynn Watt

Abandon Your Shoes

Surprise hummingbirds in day lilies
Watch a spider spin its web
Locate the swallow's nest
Watch herons fish
Scan for eagles
Collect blue jay feathers

Skip rocks
Skinny dip
Catch raindrops on your tongue
Countdown the thunder
Watch for rainbows
Imagine stories in the clouds

Eat strawberries warm with sun
Wear a crown of daisies
Build a fire on sand
Slay mosquitoes
Listen for the peepers
Wait for fireflies in the meadow

Dance

It's a dance living with you

You whistle as you stir the oatmeal pot
I strew the morning news across the bed

You jump to wash up every cup
I drop books in a jumble on the rug

You work crossword puzzles between chores
I watch pigeons promenade the gambrel roof

You tackle a hundred handy projects and read a couple books
        while I place word after word across a page
            writing to some internal tune
             to bring back mothers from their graves
        stop fathers roaming through the night
   beat back at time with rage

Until the oatmeal in its pot sits cold
The unread news is stale
Even the pigeons have flown away
And you're done dancing with a broom

Autobiography

I took my poem to the workshop —
a kind of autobiography of my life—
starting with the Sunday morning
my father drove my mother through the sleet
retracing their route of the previous night
when they ate chicken chop suey and egg foo yong
in a wooden booth lighted by a naked bulb
in a two-story walk-up eatery
it's only show piece an automated phonograph
My father says they were gay that night
the only customers   they danced to
Fred Astaire's voice crooning out
either, either, neither, neither
let's call the whole thing off
my mother was eight and a half months pregnant
this was their little joke
they never called anything off

A few hours later I shot into the world
a red and bawling preemie fueled by colic
from the womb of a mother
who did only what she could learn from books
which wasn't to nurse me or rock me or cuddle
and the spark of a father who snuggled
wherever and with whomever he could
appearing so polished and proper from the pulpit
where   without missing a beat he stood as usual
that same morning conducting the church service
omitting his first child's birth   that's me
from the list of parishioners' births   illnesses deaths
he read out each Sunday to his congregation
then he went home to sleep the whole thing off

This poem wandered on documenting my life

with idiosyncratic details adding up
to an excruciating length   it was a long poem
mine is a long and from my small perspective
an eventful life not quite over
and I used the poem
to enumerate my triumphs one by one
two marriages one bad one good
two daughters both delights doing as they should
five grandchildren no real credit to me
forty years of teaching all dedicated to my students
several books and hundreds of articles
many poems and one CD
probably none important in the broader scheme of things
and many many friends relatives gardens
dogs chickens hamsters rabbits turtles fish
and blah blah blah was this enough achievement for a life
before take-off to that Elysium Field of azure light

First I as author read the text so everyone could hear it in my voice
followed by another reader so I could hear the music and the rhythm
that reader stumbled through too many ego-driven words
followed by critiquing round the table
the title was the first to go *so mundane it doesn't pull you in*
the movement through the poem was *rough   uneven*
the rhythm *hard to pinpoint in one reading*
the form *not consistent with the meaning*
its hard to tell the purpose for which the poem was written
maybe we have two poems here or the start of three
each person so respectful of each other and the author
each with a suggestion where *to tighten up a bit*
or lop off something *not really needed*
everyone agreed they liked *the repetition of the word off*
in the last line of all four strophes
lurching through my dance toward death   which is inevitable
until the workshop mercifully ended
and I took home a simpler dirge
she lived from birth and waits for Death to fly her off

Molly Lynn Watt

Lay Abouts

They lay about the house
in hopeless disarray

No one trims their bangs
No one buys them braces
No one clips their nails
No one smiles into their faces
No one looks into their souls
No one corrects their tenses
No one checks their spelling
No one tells them where
        to break their lines
    and where to add in spaces

These orphans I have birthed
are morphing into clutter
It's time to clean them up and
make them take their places

Shadow People

About the Author

Photo credit: Daniel Lynn Watt

Molly Lynn Watt enjoyed a long career as an educator of all ages. Eight years ago she and her husband Dan moved from their lakeside home in New Hampshire to a cohousing community in Cambridge, Massachusetts where she hosts monthly Fireside Readings. She writes education books and articles, travel articles, personal essays and poems. She leads poetry workshops, served as editor for *Bagels with the Bards, Kent Street Writers Chapbook* and chair of the poetry editorial board of *HILR Review*. She with Dan Watt and Tony Saletan created *Songs and Letters of the Spanish Civil War* also available on CD, Molly reads the role of Ruth in performances.

‌‌‌‌‌‌

Colophon

This book is set in Garamond, a typeface first designed by Claude Garamond (c. 1480-1561). Garamond came to prominence in the 1540s, first for a Greek typeface he was commissioned to create for the French king Francois I, to be used in a series of books by Robert Estienne. The French court later adopted Garamond's roman types for their printing and the typeface influenced type across France and Western Europe. Garamond had likely seen Venetian old style types from the printing shops of Aldus Manutius. Garamond based much of the design of his lowercase on the handwriting of Angelo Vergecio, librarian to Francois I. The italics of most contemporary versions are based on the italics of Garamond's assistant Robert Grandjon.

Garamond's letterforms convey a sense of fluidity and consistency. Some unique characteristics in his letters are the small bowl of the a and the small eye of the e. Long extenders and top serifs have a downward slope.

Contemporary digital versions of Garamond include Adobe Garamond, Monotype Garamond, Simoncini Garamond, and Stempel Garamond. The typefaces Grandjon and Sabon (designed by Jan Tschichold), are also classified as Garamond revivals. A version called ITC Garamond, designed by Tony Stan (1917–1988) was released in 1977.

Steve Glines designed this book.

§